Simon Northouse writes fiction books designed to entertain. His stories include hefty doses of self-deprecating humour, irony, farce, and droll bathos delivered in a deadpan voice. His characters leap from the page, and the plots twist and turn as he delves into the dark alcoves of modern life and the strange things we humans do. However, as many of his fans have pointed out, there is much, much more to his books than laughter and a smattering of social commentary.

He touches on issues that have plagued humans since the first man pointed at a woman on the back of a woolly mammoth and shouted, "Oi, love, come down from there. That's a man's job!" Racism, misogyny, sexism, elitism, classism, anxiety, self-doubt, hubris and entitlement are a sprinkling of topics that intersperse his works.

Keep On Keeping On

The Discombobulated Series

Simon Northouse

Flabbergasted Publishing

simon@simonnorthouse.com or visit the Author's website at https://www.subscribepage.com/author_simon_northouse_home or Facebook page https://www.facebook.com/simonnorthouse

Disclaimer: This is a work of fiction. Names, characters, businesses, places, events, locales, and incidents are either the products of the author's imagination or used in a fictitious manner. Any resemblance to actual persons, living or dead, or actual events is purely coincidental.

Published by Flabbergasted Publishing

First Edition

Kindle e-book ISBN-13: 978-0-6485330-4-7

Paperback ISBN-13: 978-0-6485330-5-4

Contents

Keep On Keeping On

Life's a bowl of soup... grab a fork!

Book 1 of the Discombobulated Newsletter series

From the Author

Welcome to the "Discombobulated Boxset" a collection of anecdotes, reflections, true stories, and humorous musings, *(I think the reader will be the judge of that... Ed).* By the way, the person italicised in parentheses is my editor. Well, he's not really an editor, he's a good friend of mine, (acquaintance would be a better description) who thinks he's an editor. He reads everything I write to make sure I don't go over the top and cause moral outrage to millions, *(you wish... Ed)*

Sometimes, I would like to shut him up because he can be damn annoying, but it's a cross I have to bear, *(I'm still here, you know... Ed)*

The following articles have been collated from my monthly "Discombobulated" newsletter, plus some new bonus material. This is not the sort of book you'd sit down and read in one hit. It is the type of book you would peruse while sitting on a bus, or in a waiting room or maybe even on the toilet which would make it toilet humour, *(oh, no, you've started already... Ed.)* Then again, you can read it however and wherever you like. I don't care. If you enjoy it, then why not sign-up for the "Discombobulated" newsletter and get it delivered to your inbox once a month. This link will take you to my website sign-up page.

https://www.subscribepage.com/author_simon_northouse_home

Of course, if you don't like it, there's not much I can do about it at this late stage. I'll try harder next time.

All the best and keep on keeping on!

Simon Northouse

Chapter 1

Giraffes

Sometimes, when I'm trawling the internet wasting my life, I stumble across something that makes me say, "No! That cannot be true", at which point I waste more time by doing pointless investigative research (i.e. Google it).

Just such a thing happened last week. However, before I continue—a warning. The following "mildly interesting fact" contains adult giraffe content. If you are of a delicate disposition or a giraffe, you may want to skip this section.

The headline which caught my eye was this, "The female giraffe urinates in the male giraffe's mouth as part of the mating act". Call me a traditionalist, but as courtship rituals go, it's not really my cup of tea... if you get my drift. What's wrong with wearing a figure-hugging white chiffon number, a new hairdo, and a provocative fluttering of the eyelashes to get the male libido racing? Then there's the actual act itself. How the hell does she manage it? She'd have to be a bloody good shot to hit her intended target. Does the male lay under her to make it easier? Or is he happily minding his own business under a tree, finishing the cryptic crossword when next minute he's looking up at the sky thinking,

"Hmm, they didn't forecast rain today."

All pertinent questions requiring answers. Then I had a thought. Maybe the female giraffe is kinkier than she appears to be. Although, I cannot imagine her dressed in red latex thigh boots whilst gripping a riding crop between her teeth, no matter how hard I try.

If any giraffes are reading this, please don't think I am trying to ridicule your mating habits. They may be outré but I'm a firm believer in live and let live.

After exhaustive research, I finally found the truth. Although the headline was sensationalised somewhat, it is, in fact, true. If I could write book blurbs as eye-catching as that headline, I would be an international bestseller by now. So, here are some facts.

The female Giraffe only mates when she's good and ready. She will not get it on and bang her gong with any old dropkick who happens to be passing by. She wants the most suitable male to sire her child... erm... calf. A mate with strong genes, a steady job, well-groomed and one who lowers the toilet seat when finished.

When the female giraffe goes into estrus, she releases powerful pheromones which attract males. The equivalent of a spray of Chanel Grand Extrait to the cleavage for humans. It sends Gerry Giraffe wild. The male then rubs his head against the female's bum until she urinates—don't try this at home. He then tastes the urine, rather like one would a fine wine, and if the bouquet and flavour are to his liking, he tries to mount Mrs Giraffe (or Ms Giraffe–I'm not sure where giraffes sit or stand in the emancipation stakes).

Now, she likes to play hard to get. After all, she doesn't want to appear desperate. There's nothing more off-putting than a desperate female giraffe who's in season, is there? Playing hardball may include moving forward just as the male is about to mount her, (I'd call this teasing and bloody damn annoying for the male), running away to see if he follows, ignoring his phone calls or refusing to laugh at his lame jokes. If she spots a more desirable male nearby, say, one with an extensive portfolio of blue-chip shares and a Maserati, she will rub his neck with her neck to show her preference.

Finally, when she has picked her mate, usually by asking her friends what they think of him, she is ready for the deed. She stands completely still, which is a signal to the male he may proceed. Thankfully, this signal is not replicated in the human species otherwise, there'd be many unwanted pregnancies by women standing at bus stops and riding in lifts. Once the earth has moved for him, he dismounts and buggers off despite the female Giraffe wanting to talk about what colour to paint the nursery—so there are some similarities to the human species after all.

The female is in gestation for 14 ½ months by which time she can be seen staggering across the Serengeti screaming, "get this thing out of me, I've had enough!" She gives birth to her calf standing up, which to me is more astonishing than urinating in her mate's mouth. It's a long way to fall for a newborn calf and how giraffes have survived as a species is beyond me. I'm not suggesting the giraffe should be on her back, with her legs in stirrups or floating in a birthing pool, but surely there's a better way to deliver your precious cargo than letting it drop six feet to the ground—but what do I know.

The newborn is usually up and limping around with the aid of a walking stick within an hour, wondering what in hell's name has just happened. As for the male, well, let's say he's an absentee dad, and the female rears the calf herself whilst issuing court orders to the father for calf maintenance payments and bitching about him to her pals.

Here endeth this month's "Mildly Interesting Fact". One last thing, when I started this article, I told you I was searching the internet whereupon I came across the above mind-boggling headline. I know what you are thinking, and you're wrong! I was not looking for giraffe porn! I'd actually typed into Google the phrase, "fact is stranger than fiction"... honest.

One last thing; I've just ordered a giraffe online. Not sure if it will be delivered though, I was told it's a tall order.

Chapter 2

Ants In The Pants

I 've had a torrid couple of weeks. Firstly, I've been suffering from tennis elbow, and I don't even play tennis and secondly, last week I had a centipede take up residence in my underpants... while I was still in them—stop laughing—it isn't funny!

As I flopped out of bed the other morning, I felt a movement in my jocks. At first, I assumed it was the usual suspect, as I was half-asleep. However, I soon realised this was not a natural sensation; it was a wriggly, squiggly feeling. There's only one thing faster than the speed of light, and it's a man taking off his Y-fronts when he suspects a creepy-crawly is within striking distance of his family jewels. Not only that, but the malevolent little bugger had taken a couple of bites out of me. Luckily, my three sentinels in the Rapid Response Unit were unscathed, but it was a damn close call that could have resulted in serious swelling—which—could have been a blessing.

My first reaction was, "How the hell did a centipede get into my undies?" Initially, I thought it might have been a macabre practical joke played by my wife. However, a centipede is not her style—a tarantula or scorpion—yes, but not a centipede.

I'm a man with an inquisitive nature so I conducted some extensive research (Google, again) on centipedes which leads neatly on to this month's mildly interesting fact.

Despite the name, centipedes can never have exactly 100 legs. Why? Because they always have an odd number *(I'd say having that number of legs is bloody odd to start with—Ed).* They can have 99 or 101 legs but never 100, as it's an even number. Of course, they could have 100 legs if they'd lost one leg in a lawn mowing accident, I guess.

Using the internet to find out exactly how many legs a centipede possesses has proved confusing. As there are over eight thousand distinct species, this is hardly surprising. Some people say anywhere between 15 and 427, but 177 seems to crop up the most.

Centipedes are rarely seen during daylight hours as they spend most of the day in the bathroom clipping their toenails. They venture out at night looking for food and a good podiatrist. Their food of choice is meat, as I'm acutely aware, and they'll eat practically anything, including other insects, earthworms, slugs, dead rodents, and even discarded KFC... I know, it's hard to believe.

Now here's a weird thing. Reproduction for the centipede does not involve copulation, which to me is the best part of reproduction. I think someone needs to have a quiet word in the male centipede's ear and tell him he's missing a trick. I won't go into too much detail about the reproductive process as some of you may be eating, but I'll give you a quick overview.

Let's say, the male centipede takes things into his own hands or, in his case, feet, until he hits the jackpot. The more sophisticated centipede, (let's call him Raphael) will then leave his jackpot on the web of Mrs Centipede, who may or may not be amused by his offering, depending on what sort of day she's had at the office. If she's in the mood, she will embrace Raphael's deposit, and this will fertilise her egg. However, the less sophisticated male centipede, (we'll call him Dave) leaves his jackpot in any old place in the off-chance Mrs Centipede treads in it—which, with that many legs, is a distinct possibility.

So why did a centipede take up lodgings in my underpants? Apparently, they like somewhere warm and moist to curl up in to get a good day's sleep. I guess my undergarments meet those criteria. They also like to be safe and find a hidey-hole where they are unlikely to be disturbed. Once again, my undies pass that test with flying colours.

It is possible my jocks fell from the washing line and a passing centipede saw them as the arthropods equivalent of the Sky Villa at The Palms Resort. However, for that to be true, it would have meant my many-legged friend had been camping out for nearly twenty-four hours at Northouse HQ. It's conceivable but unlikely.

Excluding my wife and the camping theory, it leaves only one alternative. The little devil must have burrowed in as I slept. I only hope it was a female centipede and not a male looking for a bit of solo fun.

You may wonder what happened to the centipede *(no, not really—Ed.)* Did I kill him or her? The answer is no. Centipedes are excellent at killing other insects, such as spiders, silverfish, moths, and mosquitoes. I like to think of Mr (or hopefully Mrs) Centipede as my personal security guard, keeping me safe from a whole host of other nasties. But if the centipede goes off-piste again and crosses the border into the land of leaks and peaks, he's going to be an ex-centipede.

Lastly, here's another proven fact; did you know that if you are bitten in the groin by a centipede, you won't sing "Magic Moments" by Perry Como for over a month.

Chapter 3

The Gloat Email

I look forward to Christmas for many reasons. Eating, drinking, sleeping, arguing with the wife as we try to manoeuvre the Christmas tree into its stand, and making disparaging remarks about the Von Trapp's singing ability.

However, there is one thing I do not enjoy—the yearly Christmas "gloat" email from people I once worked with for a few weeks back in 1994. I have three people who send me these festive missives, Bob, Karen, and someone who refers to themselves simply as "Z". I cannot ever recall working or knowing anyone whose first or last name began with Z. Maybe at some point, I've exchanged email addresses with Mark Zuckerberg, Jay-Z or Zoe Ball but I don't really move in those circles—well, not anymore.

The emails give me a recap of their year, their perfect year—may I add. They gush about their gifted children, their expensive overseas trips, their work promotions. They also contain interesting nuggets of information such as, "on June 15th I had boiled eggs for breakfast with one slice of multi-grain toast." I'm not sure how I've survived this long without knowing that. In fact, now I think of it, their emails are a bit like this newsletter—WTF! *(You're not wrong there, mate—Ed.)*

I never usually reply as I don't want to encourage the buggers. However, this year, I composed my own "year of reflection" to stick it back to them, with spades. However, when my wife read my email, she said,

"Don't even think about hitting the send button—you idiot!" My reply was, "Guess what, my sweetness and light, I will let my newsletter subscribers decide, so suck on that pipe!" She responded with something like, "W**K*R!" My hearing is not the best these days, for reasons you may have already ascertained.

Here is my draft email. If I receive overwhelming support to send it, then I can enjoy a guilt free piece of schadenfreude to enjoy over Christmas.

Dear Bob, Karen, and Z,

even though you do not know each other, I am replying en masse as I can't be arsed to write to each of you individually—after all, life is short, or at least it appears that way after reading your emails.

It's amazing to think three such disparate people have so much in common. You are all super successful, (which really is astonishing as, Bob and Karen, when I knew you, you were bottom of the food chain and sinking fast—and Z—I don't even know who the hell you are). Apparently, you all have children who are "gifted" and "beautiful". I'm sorry, Bob, but I think you may be gilding the Lilly slightly there. As I recall, if it's the correct Bob, you looked like the half-cousin of Quasimodo after a hard night on the bells. I cannot imagine your daughter is a younger version of Nicole Kidman, as you claim if she was sired from your spawn.

Anyway, I'd love to shake each one of you warmly by the throat and here is my email reflecting on my year—for a change.

WOW! What a year!!!!! My, how time flies. It seems like only twelve months ago since I was sitting here reading your self-obsessed, vainglorious twaddle. Now it's time for my egotistical ramblings.

On 30th December 2017, I married my long-suffering life partner, Mavis. It was a very special day as not only did we tie the knot, but I also found my precious Swiss Army Penknife stuck behind the bar fridge in the shed! Imagine my surprise. It was the highlight of the day. Everyone laughed and laughed, well, almost everyone.

We had so many guests I lost count after five. My, how they ate and drank, and ate and drank, and ate and drank. Of course, it is a once in a lifetime occasion, (fingers crossed ha, ha,) so I wasn't counting the cost (£154.89 - excluding the ice). However, I must admit it slightly miffed me when I found out some rotter helped themself to a few bottles from my vintage wine collection of Merda Vino 2018. At £0.49 per bottle, it's not something to be swilled like beer! I never caught the culprit, (good job I didn't! I was bloody ropeable on the day). However, Mavis's mother was particularly happy and boisterous on the night, which was somewhat out of character for her—not that I'm pointing an accusatory finger (I still have the scars from the last time I made that mistake).

We received many lovely gifts we will treasure for a while. I didn't know you could get such quality at the £1 Shop.

Not long after the wedding, I had a terrible accident when I snicked my cuticle while clipping my big toenail. Unless you have experienced this traumatic and life-changing event, you have absolutely no idea what pain is. Give me childbirth any day of the week! However, I was rather puzzled by the paramedic's less than sympathetic attitude. I immediately lodged a formal complaint with the hospital and justice was swiftly administered. They were stood down for two weeks without pay.

Yes, I know you all want to hear about my work life. Well, nothing much has changed there. I'm steering the ship, managing my workload and everyone else's, cutting costs, raising profits, and smashing all the benchmarks I set last year. I'm still the Senior Manager, although my title of "Office Clerk" doesn't truly reflect the enormity of my responsibilities or my natural genius for the role. However, I'm not one to quibble over titles, although I would prefer it if people referred to me as "Sir" rather than the more informal, noggin. (I must Google the word noggin and find out its meaning. I'm sure it must be Nordic for king or warrior leader or such like).

My eldest daughter, Cleetoris, will start at the (exclusive) Grammar School this year (we had to decline the Scholarship to King's College, as she didn't like the colour of the school uniform). As you will be aware, scholarships are awarded only to the most gifted and intelligent children. My, oh my, it was a tough test. Over seven hundred applicants from all over the country turned up for it. I really didn't think Cleetoris had a chance, but as usual, she astounded me by getting 99.9% in the test and came top. I told her not to get complacent; 99.9% is good, but there's still plenty of scope for improvement. She is looking forward to it with great excitement and anticipation. Every night when I pass her room, I hear her sobs of joy and the words "Oh, the Grammar, the Grammar, why me?"

On a rather sad note... Cleetoris has given up the piano!!!! I can hear your collective gasps and groans. I know, I know, it is a tragedy! It truly is a significant loss to the music world, and I think we should stop for a minute's silence:

Where did it all go wrong? To be fair to Cleetoris, I had some sympathy for her. Once she had mastered the complete works of Mozart, Beethoven, Chopin, Schubert, and Barry Manilow, she asked herself the question Alexander the Great asked himself after he'd conquered the known world, "Where to now? There's nothing left". I endured a similar experience as a boy of 28 when I finally mastered the Rubik's Cube after fifteen years of trying.

Her music teacher (ha, that's a contradiction in terms) had to be sedated for two days on hearing the news. I told Cleetoris she should start composing her own works, something with a bit more depth than the classics (I always found Mozart a little twee for my tastes). Alas, you can lead a horse to water, but you can't pass an eye through a camel's needle. Anyway, she's taken up the harp and viola and is already better than her tutor (who is ex-Philharmonic Symphony).

My Great Uncle Charlie, (whom none of you know) had a bunion operated on last week. I'm sure you'll all join me in wishing him the best.

The morning of May 12th was not a good one. As I got out of bed, I stubbed my big toe. I immediately had a giddy turn and had to lie down in a darkened room with a wet flannel over my forehead for three hours. I received scant sympathy from my wife, Mavis.

Unfortunately, during the year I had an argument with my local butcher when I questioned the girth of his sausage. Things became heated rather quickly. I would rather not talk about it, as I still carry the mental scars to this day. Mavis had a devil of a job removing the sausage stains from my underwear.

On June 16th, I changed the fan belt on the Toyota Hilux. Modern engines are now all computerised and extraordinarily complex. They are only supposed to be worked on by the most experienced of mechanics. However, being a bit of a handyman, I tackled the job myself. I quickly speed-read the 800-page manual and thirty minutes later, Bob's your uncle, Aunts your fanny—fanbelt fitted. I also tweaked the turbo-injectors while I was at it and replaced the big end.

We holidayed at Grimesore Bottom this year, which for those of you who haven't visited, is rather like Tuscany but with drive-through off-licences and heroin injecting rooms. We had a wonderful time making fun of the locals. Unfortunately, it was marred by the engine blowing up on the Toyota Hilux. Let me tell you, Toyota HQ would have been quaking in their boots the day they opened my letter! We settled out of court (I'm not a litigious person) and I'm now the proud owner of a Toyota drinks bottle and keyring. (I've actually attached the keyring to my Swiss Army Knife, as I'm a bit of a joker—ha, ha!)

Daughter number 2, Vaginna, was made Student of the Year at kindergarten. I've told her she needs to hide her talents under a bushel a little more as she's making all the other kids look like real thickos. She asked me what a bushel was—she's such a prankster.

I think some of the other parents have developed a touch of the green-eyed monster, as they seem to avoid me when I go to collect her. It can't be easy spawning extremely average children, but let me tell you, it's no walk in the park trying to keep up with two outrageously gifted daughters either.

I had some bad news from overseas during the year. My best mate from primary school, "Sludgebucket" was killed in a combine-harvester accident. I haven't actually spoken or written to him for over 35 years, but he will always be with me. I intended to send a wreath to his family but couldn't for the life of me remember his real name (what a klutz, ha, ha!) Mavis didn't think it appropriate to deliver a wreath to grieving parents that read, "Sludgebucket RIP". I couldn't see a problem with it, but Mavis is a little more tactful than I on these matters.

In June, Mavis spent three days in the gynaecological unit of the local hospital. Luckily, it was not contagious, and I escaped unscathed (phew!!!!)

On September 6th, we had a family outing to Kmart. The weather was fantastic, and I bought myself a new state-of-the-art plasma TV, a new iBook, and a new set of golf clubs. Mavis got herself a heavy-duty treadmill and a new girdle. However, the trip was marred by unacceptable behaviour from the girls. They asked if they could have something as well. You know me and there's no way I'll stand for that self-obsessed, materialistic, me-me-me attitude. After screaming at them for ten minutes and publicly humiliating them, I think they saw the error of their ways. I told them there would be no more family excursions for the foreseeable future if this is the thanks I get.

On the sporting front, we've tried to curtail some of the children's activities. The head scout for the British Olympic Committee put pressure on us to send Cleetoris to the Olympic Summer School during the holidays, but we stood our ground. We felt training for the 100m, 200m,

400m, 800m and 1500m in both swimming and running and the javelin, long jump, triathlon, archery, equestrian, not to mention the Marathon, was a tad too much.

As for Vaginna, she was invited to train with the English Women's Cricket Team to prepare for the next world cup. I can't help feeling that at six years old, she is a little young to be competing competitively. They'll just have to do without her batting average of 199.7.

On October 24th, I cleaned out my shed and went to the tip. Mavis slept late until 11 am and we rounded the day off nicely with a bowl of my handmade pasta and my homemade rabbit cheese (it's not easy milking rabbits, I can tell you).

Mavis has gone from strength to strength in her job and I can see the day very shortly when she'll be Head Principal. She can then start implementing her lifelong plan to revolutionise the entire education system (which is long overdue, may I add!) Her relentless discourse to the Minister for Education seems to have fallen on deaf eyes. There's none as blind as those who can't hear. However, until then she'll struggle valiantly on as assistant cleaner at Crudthorpe College.

She's now Team Leader at weight watchers and practically runs the meetings. She has lost an incredible 22 kg during the year and only gained 24 kg in return. I think it's a sterling effort and it won't be long before she'll be able to walk without serious chaffing to her inner thighs and buttocks.

Did I mention Cleetoris has taken up sculpture? Well, she has. I wasn't impressed with her first attempt, as it was a replica of Michelangelo's "David". To be honest, it was far superior to the original, but that's not the point I'm trying to make. I told her, "There's no room for plagiarism in this house". Thankfully, she heeded the message and is now working on a giant slab of marble, chiselling out the complete DNA helix of the Patagonian Dragonfly. A little obvious, I know, but at least it's her own work.

On November 30th I paid a visit to the local pharmacy to buy some Anusol as my piles have returned with a raging vengeance. I also picked up an extra-large box of panty pads for Mavis.

Well, that's all I have time for at the moment. I must dash as I am giving a headline speech at the Royal Society of Shovel Admirers this evening. It should prove to be a fascinating night as my soliloquy examines the evolution of the shovel, followed by a health and safety talk on how to turn sods correctly and lastly, the importance of having a well-oiled shaft.

We really must stay connected more often and anytime you're passing, please call in as we love visitors dropping in unannounced.

All the best from Northouse Mansions and my sincerest sympathy to you all. Go in peace.

Chapter 4

English Versus American

It's been a hectic month with the release of a new book, working on the next one, marketing the damned things and trying to find out what was causing a revolting smell in my fridge.

Let's start with the important matters first. You'll be pleased to know I found out what was causing the eye-watering, gut-churning smell or maybe you don't really give a toss. Anyway, after forensic analysis, I eventually found the culprit—cauliflower rice. For reasons best known to herself, my wife has become obsessed with cauliflower rice. What is wrong with "rice" rice? Two packets in the crisper were only a month past their sell-by date, which in our house usually means, "Ah, it'll be all right." Not on this occasion! After I had donned radioactive personal protection, gas mask, Geiger counter and extinguished all naked flames, I removed the life-threatening culprits from the fridge and deposited them in the outside bin.

However, as I write this, bin collection is still two days away, and it is damned hot outside. My nearest neighbour lives about two miles away and he called around this morning to ask if I had noticed a "violent miasma in the air." I feigned ignorance and declared I had noticed nothing untoward —which is hard to do while holding your breath. The only positive to take from this is the bin will walk itself down the driveway in a couple of days, so saving me the trouble.

Okay, so let's quickly move on to this month's "Mildly Interesting Fact".

I occasionally receive emails from kind people who tell me there is a spelling error in one of my books. I appreciate this as I'm always looking for perfection, *(but surprisingly, never finding it—Ed)*. However, on most occasions, it is not a spelling error but the difference between "British" English and "American" English.

Being a native-born Yorkshire man and therefore English and also British and a citizen of the United Kingdom and the British Isles and a member of the Commonwealth (it's complicated), I speak and write in British English. In fact, it was only with the advent of Microsoft Windows in the early nineties I became aware there was such a thing as American English. Until that time, I assumed there was only English English.

Microsoft Word would always let me know when I had misspelt (or misspelled) "colour", indicating it is spelt (or spelled) "color". It would also get annoyed with me for "specialising" instead of "specializing", or for using the unit of measurement known around the world as "metre" instead of meter. It once even picked me up for spelling "socks" incorrectly, insisting the correct spelling was indeed, "sox"—proving Microsoft and computers have a sense of humour or humor, as obviously, no one would ever spell socks as sox.

This got me thinking, *(always a bad sign—Ed)*, about the British and Americans. We have much in common and yet—we are very different.

One of the biggest differences is our units of measurement. Britain used the imperial system until the early seventies. When we joined the Common Market (think European Union), we converted to metric (reluctantly). Gone were pounds and ounces, miles, and feet, square yards, shillings, groats, fathoms, and tons. These were replaced with grams, kilograms, metres, and centimetres. In addition, we had a new decimal currency, which has 100 pence (pennies) in a pound (instead of the more logical 240?). However, it has never sat comfortably with the nation. We still serve beer in pints, not litres. We fill our cars up in gallons and we still curse in imperial.

"He's a six-foot waste of space."

"I'll bet you a pound to a penny of shit he's wrong!" and

"He's a few bob short of a shilling."

The USA employs the imperial system of measurement, but here is a "mildly interesting fact". In the US (and I think Canada) a ton is equal to 2000 pounds, whereas, in Britain, a ton is equal to 2240 pounds. These differences in units of measurement are easy to sort out by using an online converter.

Where the real confusion lies is in our use of language—which, if you haven't fallen asleep by now—is where I started.

Talking of Canadians, I once had an American tell me a Canadian was simply an American without a sense of humour—a bit harsh, I thought. That was until I spent two weeks on a coaching—camping holiday around the outback of Australia (not Austria) in the company of two Canadians. They weren't miserable by any means, but I did not see them laugh once during the fortnight! I found this most peculiar as there's a lot to laugh at whilst on a coaching holiday in Australia—the Australians for starters *(oops, there go all your Australian and Canadian subscribers—Ed)*. No, really, I love the Australians. They have a great sense of humour and can laugh at themselves and the British, well, mainly the British. They also change their Prime Minister more often than I change my underwear, which probably says more about me than it does about them.

Okay, so where was I? Ah yes, that's right, I've just lost all my Canadian and Australian subscribers and now I'll probably lose all my American ones.

Let me start at the top by beginning at the bottom. In the States, a "fanny" is a colloquial term for a bottom, behind, buttocks. However, in Britain, a fanny is not a bottom. It's pretty damn close to a bottom, and I must confess it is a very pleasant place to visit, although I don't get there as often as I'd like. So, if you're an American visiting Britain, I would advise against using the following statements in public places in case you are arrested.

"Here, hand me the cucumber, I'll stick it in my fanny pack."

"If you don't stop messing around young lady, you'll get a smacked fanny!"

"I'm sorry officer, but all I did was slap my wife on the fanny..." at which point you'll be handcuffed and thrown into the back of a divvy wagon (police van) and whisked away. I think by now you may understand what a fanny is in the UK.

Here's a statement for you, "I'm pissed!" Americans reading this will assume I am extremely annoyed, maybe even angry. The British will look at their watches, and think,

"Bloody hell, he's started a bit early, hasn't he? I think he has a drinking problem." Brits, when pissed, are usually found staggering down the high street at 2 am singing "Oh what a lovely bunch of coconuts", whilst eating a kebab and looking for someone to fight.

In Britain, we wee. In the States, they pee. We wee in a toilet unless we're pissed, then we wee in a shop doorway. Americans do their peeing in a bathroom or "John". I'm not entirely sure how John reacts to this, but I assume he's used to it by now.

In Britain, our normal greeting is "all right" usually said as "arite". Although, in Yorkshire, we use a mixture of "arite" and "eh up", as we are slightly more sophisticated than the rest of the country. The Americans seem to use, "Hi, how are you doing?" as their preferred greeting. I would advise against using this term in the UK as you may get a, "What the bloody hell has it got to do with you?" thrown back in your face. I would also stay away from the greeting, "Howdy" as you will either be laughed at or the person you said it to will begin a bad impersonation of John Wayne.

Unlike Americans, the Brits rarely complain, even when the service or food is appallingly bad, which is most of the time. We vent our spleen by whispering to our partner in the restaurant,

"Well, we won't be coming here again, thank you very much!" When asked by the waiter if everything is "arite," we reply,

"Yes, yes, it's all fine, wonderful, thanks". The Brits also talk quietly in public places unless we are pissed, then we get an overwhelming desire to speak at American volume, i.e. deafening. Although to be fair, most Americans I have met have been from Texas or New York—if I spoke to someone, from say, Wisconsin or Idaho, would I still need to wear double hearing protection?

America's head of state (The President) is democratically elected by the people every four years and can only serve a maximum of two terms, presumably to stop the abuse of power—a wise move. However, the British head of state is based on genealogy and gender and inherits the position from their parents (i.e. the King or Queen). There is no election process, no democratic voting, and they hold the position for life, unless they do something foolish, like marrying an American divorcee, at which point they will be forced to abdicate and the next in "line" will take up the mantle.

Of course, the US President is not only the head of state but also the head of government and wields enormous power. In fact, it is probably the most powerful position in the world. The Queen of England, Britain, and the Commonwealth does not really have any power. She is part of what is called a constitutional monarchy.

The British have a peculiar tendency to insist on using utensils to eat their food. For our American cousins, let me explain. These utensils replace the fingers and are called, "knife, fork, and spoon". Each one has a different use and I'm sure if you've ever visited Britain then you may have spotted these strange looking objects in restaurants, sorry, diners.

In Britain, we have servings of small, medium, and large. In America, there is no direct equivalent to the British small—it does not exist. They have regular (i.e. British large), large and extra-large. In fact, I figure (or reckon) that in the next twenty years, the word "small" will have disappeared from the American language—and British English will be called American American.

Let's talk about herbs. The British pronounce the "H" in herbs. As in "Herbie Goes To Monte Carlo". If it were meant to be pronounced "erbs" it would be spelt "erbs". The same assessment goes for "oregano" (or-eee-gar-no) and "basil" (baaz-ill)—not "o-regin-no" or "bay-zil".

When it comes to cars (or automobiles), things get really confusing. Brits call it a gear stick, not a shift stick. A bonnet is a hood, a boot is a trunk, and a bumper is a fender. However, a bonnet is also knitted headwear, and a trunk can be a valise, or suitcase, or part of a tree or an elephant's nose, or a euphemism for a penis. If someone asks you,

"Would you like to see my elephant impression?" Politely decline and walk away.

A boot is also a type of footwear, and we also boot a footy ball and we can also get a boot to the balls, usually when we are pissed, at 2 am, looking for a fight, eating a kebab and singing—"Oh what a lovely bunch..." well, you get the picture.

The Americans "hood" could also refer to a gangster or your neighbourhood or neighborhood. Our gangster is also a gangster, but we call him the taxman.

I'm not sure if Americans have an unhealthy preoccupation with the weather, but in Britain, we do. We talk about the weather constantly, which is surprising really, as for 363 days of the year it is grey (gray) skies with a touch of drizzle and a bit on the "chilly side". When Britain has a scorching summer, (e.g. 3 continuous days of 27°C / 81°F) the entire country goes into party mode. We use it as another excuse to get pissed.

The British have a good understanding of geography. We know the difference between Austria and Australia, Japan and China, Myanmar and

Burma. I think this innate knowledge of the countries of the world stems from the fact that at some point in our history we invaded at least one-third of them. Of course, in those days, it wasn't called invasion. It was rather quaintly known as colonisation—although I'm not sure the locals saw it that way.

The Americans don't do invasion, they do liberation, but not as well as the Brits used to do colonisation. However, Americans are smart! They realised a long time ago there's no point taking over a country unless you are going to make a dollar out of it—so they did it with their business acumen. What country in the world does not have an Apple Mac, an MS Office program, an iPad, an Intel processor? I would bet every nation on the planet has a Harley Davidson, a Jeep, a Ford, or a GM car powering down their roads right now. Which country in the world does not use Google, Amazon, and Facebook, eat from a MacDonald's, KFC, Dunkin' Donuts, or get a coffee from a Starbucks. I won't even touch on Hollywood, Netflix, Fox, or M.A.S.H.

The Americans conquered the world via the backdoor and made a very healthy profit doing so. How do the British compare? Well, over the last fifty years we have given the world—erm, erm, ah yes! We have given the world Dyson vacuum cleaners and Gordon Ramsay, so we are nearly on par.

Enough of the differences, let's look at the similarities between the two nations.

The Brits gave you, The Beatles, The Stones, The Who, The Kinks, Oasis, Rod Stewart, and Elton John. In return, the Americans gave us Chuck Berry, Elvis, Bob Dylan, Otis Redding, Sam Cook, The Doors, Motown, Eminem, The Byrds, and Mariah Carey (thanks for that).

The differences are many—but the similarities are greater still. I hope you have taken this as it was intended—a bit of tongue-in-cheek banter—

and if not, tough titty, and I think that particular phrase is common to both British and American English.

Thought to self: *Okay, let me count up. I'll lose all Canadian subscribers because they don't have a sense of humour. I'll lose both Australians because they hate the Poms (British) anyway, and I'll lose at least 600 Americans because they just love subscribing and unsubscribing. I'll also lose 3 British subs because they came home pissed and didn't know what they were doing. That leaves the guy from South Africa, the Lady-boy from Indonesia (I'll PM you soon—promise) and Snorg from Norway—so all good, onwards and upwards.*

Chapter 5

Remember the Days of the Old School Yard

W elcome to the Marbruary edition of the Discombobulated Newsletter.

"What medication is this guy on?" I hear you exclaim. What the hell is Marbruary? Well, it's a mash-up of March and February. It's a new month I've invented so I can meet my deadlines without feeling defeated. Aw, come on, cut me some slack here. Anyway, count your blessings. I was considering calling it "Farch" which sounds like a disgusting sexual practice *(and if it isn't, then it should be—Ed).*

Note to self: Google the word "farch" before hitting the send button otherwise, I could have 600 morally outraged readers hitting unsubscribe. For crying out loud! What is wrong with the world? Okay, forget I ever mentioned Farch.

Time seems to be passing at an exponential rate. Do you realise it's only 10 months until Xmas? Thought that would cheer you up. So, what have I been up to since we last spoke? Well, I published the second instalment of The School Reports in early Feb. This is a humorous peek back to yesteryear when teachers were... how can I put this nicely... when they were more "robust" in their report writing. In fact, they were more robust at everything.

These were the days when schools were run like schools, i.e. prison camps, unlike today where they are more like multinational corporations. Reading my own children's reports these days means having on hand a copy of the "Dictionary Of Wank Words" to help me decipher exactly what the teacher is trying to say. Does anyone know what "horizontal integration" means? I assumed it meant lying down on the floor during a school assembly—but apparently not.

I'm certainly not having a dig at teachers. They must have one of the hardest jobs on the planet dealing with tantrums, subterfuge, aggression, and truculence—and that's just from the parents and other teachers.

As I wrote "The School Reports" it brought back a lot of memories from my school days which got me thinking about how much things have changed. This led me to do a bit of research via the big "G" in the sky (I mean Google, not God. Although, some people would say they are the same thing; omnipotent, omnipresent, omniscient, and omnidirectional—that's a lot of omnis for one newsletter, which is ominous). Anyway, I digress. This month's "Mildly Interesting Fact" is all about the old school days. So, let us take a trip back in time and revisit what it was actually like in the 50s, 60s, 70s, and 80s.

Here's a mildly interesting fact: "Margaret Thatcher" was a woman. Now, as facts go, that one is pretty lame. It's like saying water is wet. For those who have never heard of Mrs T, she was the first British female prime minister, coming to power in 1979 until her own party deposed her in 1990. However, well before then, she came to prominence in 1970 as Secretary of State for Education and Science. She became rather unpopular, as one of her first acts was to abolish the "free" milk program for 7 to 11 year olds. This got her the nickname Thatcher the Milk Snatcher.

When I started school, they gave us a small bottle of milk at morning playtime (recess), about a third of a pint. My greatest ambition was to become a milk monitor, an ambition never fulfilled and still rankles with me to this day. The milk monitor would depart about twenty minutes before playtime and would collect the empty bottles afterwards, meaning he would miss a good hour of the school day. I say "he", as yes, in those days there was a clear demarcation about what was appropriate for each gender.

These were also the days of corporal punishment. I'm sure many of you will remember this, but for those who are a lot younger and don't fully understand the concept—let me explain. Corporal punishment involved a fully grown man or woman beating the shit out of a defenceless small child with impunity.

I well remember the day I was caught fighting with another boy in the school playground. Unfortunately, Mr Crowbottom (I kid you not) was on yard duty. Old Birdbum (as he was known to the kids) was the fearsome headmaster who ruled with an iron rod. He marched us to his office by twisting and dragging us by the ears. If you've never had your ear twisted sharply, try it one day, it's great fun.

I knew we would both be getting the cane or the slipper. However, old Birdbum was a master of psychological warfare. He wouldn't take us into his office and quickly lecture us, then dole out the punishment—oh no! That would be too quick. He made us wait in his reception room until playtime was over, by which time he would have rounded up at least another ten boys for some petty misdemeanours. These could range from swearing, fighting, accidental damage to school property, chewing gum, or even picking your nose in public.

The waiting was the worst. For some boys, it was their first time, and they would sit, sweating, with tears rolling down their cheeks, asking if it was going to hurt. There was one lad called Jimmy Broadbent who was older than me, and I reckon he spent more time in the reception room than he did studying in class. He was an old hand, and it was always heartening to see his happy, smiling face. He would laugh, joke around, and do Birdbum impressions to get everyone laughing as we awaited the inevitable.

When we were finally summoned into his office, he would make us stand rigidly with our hands by our sides, as if we were in the army. He would light a cigarette (yes, I know, hard to believe now), sit in his chair and eye us both silently for a few seconds. Birdbum never wanted to know the whys and wherefores of a situation. No, he would jump straight to his summation and sentencing. I remember the exact words he said that day, the irony of which did not pass me by even though I was only nine years old. He said, "This school and society will not tolerate violent and aggressive behaviour." He stood, grabbed his slipper from a draw, bent us over and gave us six of the best on the backside. As I walked from the room, smarting, I remember thinking, "And who's going to give that bastard the slipper for his violent and aggressive behaviour".

If you have never been whacked on the arris by an old slipper, why not try it. Just ask your local neighbourhood sadist to administer the punishment and I can guarantee that you will not use the phrase, "Hmm, I fancy a pickled onion with that", for over a week.

We were lucky it was the slipper. It could have been the cane. The pain from a slipper thrashing dissipates in a few minutes, whereas the pain of the cane would last hours. That was a formally organised punishment administered by a kangaroo court. However, my class teachers delivered less formal punishment swiftly. This could include a slap to the head, the dreaded ear twist, the ruler to an outstretched palm or worse to the back of the knuckles; the blackboard ruler to the back of the thighs, the blackboard rubber thrown at the head, and almost every teacher had a slipper in their desk drawer.

I cannot recall a female teacher using corporal punishment. Instead, they would go next door and ask a male teacher to administer the pain. I always found this odd. After all, if you've decided to hurt a small child, at least have the guts to do it yourself instead of using a proxy.

There was another form of punishment which was much worse than the physical ones—humiliation! Ah yes, there's nothing like a good dose of humiliation in front of your giggling peers to put you on the straight and narrow. Mr Selko, also known as "Psycho" was a master of humiliation. On rare occasions, he would take us for physical education when the sports teacher was off sick. He insisted the boys remove their underwear before putting their shorts on. (The same rule didn't apply to the girls regarding their underwear, probably because they wore skirts.) He was some sort of cleanliness nut-job and said that getting sweaty underpants was disgusting. He would take all the girls and boys outside, line the boys up against one wall, and the girls would line up opposite, with both genders were facing each other.

He'd slowly walk down the line of boys and slip his finger behind the elastic of our shorts, pull it back and peer down, checking we were not wearing any underwear (I know, weird right?) I remember the day one poor lad had either not heard the instructions correctly or wasn't aware of Psycho's tactics. The boy was made to take three paces forward, drop his shorts, and remove his underwear in front of a bunch of giggling girls. His face was understandably as red as a beetroot. Rest assured, if Psycho ever took us for PE, I made damn sure my jocks were resting safely back in the changing rooms.

I suppose the tactics teachers used in those days were similar to Pavlov's Dog theory. Whenever Pavlov fed his dog, he would constantly ring a bell. After a time, all he had to do was ring the bell and the dog would begin salivating. The dog had been conditioned to associate the sound of the bell with food. If you substitute the bell with physical or mental punishment, you have a similar situation—a deterrent.

This was the mid-seventies and the height of the baby boomers, so schools and classrooms were heaving under the weight of so many children. Forty-plus to a classroom was not unusual at my junior school, which probably had over five hundred kids attending. Punishment was employed to keep the pot from boiling over, and no one gave it a second thought. It was the norm. In fact, on the rare occasions, I got into trouble, I would try to hide it from my parents. If I had told them I had received the slipper or cane, they would have been incensed—not at the teachers—but at me!

I well remember my mother finding out about some minor indiscretion of mine, (talking in class) for which I'd received a hefty whack to the back of the knuckles on my left hand (always the left hand for right-handers, that way you could still hold a pen). As I explained my version of events, I recall her words vividly.

"Hmm, well, you must have been doing something wrong? Teachers don't hit you for nothing." When my father got home and my mother had grassed me up, he would gaze at me in a weary, disappointed way and say,

"Well lad, I hope you've learnt your bloody lesson?" I had friends whose parents weren't as easygoing as mine and they would receive another dose of corporal punishment. The teachers were never in the wrong!

Reading this back, it seems archaic, even barbaric, but as mentioned earlier—this was the norm; it was how things were done. If it makes my school days seem like hell on earth, it could not be further from the truth. My junior school days were some of the best days of my life and I look back on them fondly and still laugh at some of the events that took place.

Those days taught me some invaluable life lessons. The well-worn clichés of, "The school of hard knocks" and "The University of Life" hold some truth. I learnt to avoid psychos. Keep away from the "bad lads" who were always in trouble because you'd be tarred with the same brush. Circumnavigate the bullies; remove yourself completely from the manipulators and those who play mind games. Choose your friends carefully and lastly, always remove your underwear before performing any strenuous sporting activity, lest you be paraded naked down the high street.

For those of you who lived through those times, you will relate to some of this. For those of you who are younger, you will probably think it is far-fetched nonsense. I can assure you it's not far-fetched at all, it only deviates slightly from the truth. Well, my truth at least.

Chapter 6

Flasher Alert

The other day, I came across a new type of fiction called Flash Fiction. Apparently, it's all the rage (in a good sense). It's for people who are standing in queues (the British), and those who are doing short commutes (i.e. those on their way to jail or work—the same thing I guess.) These books (?) can be read in a few seconds.

Inspired, I wrote my own piece of Flash Fiction. I have reproduced it here for your delectation.

"Gone, In A Flash, Gordon" by Simon Northouse

Once upon a time, on a dark stormy night, everyone lived happily ever after. Apart from Gordon, who was "had up" for exposing himself in a public space often frequented by small furry animals and elderly ladies suffering from chronic lumbago.

The End.

The book is the first of a 5000 book series, tentatively titled, "The Curious Misadventures Of Gordon Flashman". I competitively priced each book at $10.99. I will create box sets containing a hundred books in each. These will have a page count of at least 10 and will be priced lower than buying the books individually. I like to give value for money. I aim to finish book 4999 by tomorrow night. Just in case anyone took this the wrong way—I'm joking, it's not £10.99, it's £9.99.

Chapter 7

In A Reverie

I used to assume the Latin phrase; "Tempus Fugit" was a swear term meaning "Please go away right now!" (I'm being polite.)

'Oi, Maximus, put that sword down; you'll have someone's bloody eye out! Now, tempus fugit!'

'Tempus fugit to you too, pal! Bloody Spartans! They think they run the joint!'

However, it actually means "Time Flies", and that is what this month's Mildly Interesting Fact is about.

Now, I'm no scientist but it doesn't stop me from thinking I am. I've been pondering the make-up of the universe lately, which makes a change from me pondering which colour socks I should wear each day.

There is something inherently wrong with how the universe works, in particular, how time works. Bear with me; I will not go deep here, mainly because I don't really have a clue what I'm talking about.

Have you noticed when you do boring tasks time slows down? When you sweep the yard, paint a fence, or watch an episode of Downton Abbey, the damn clock barely moves. Yet, the opposite is true when you are enjoying yourself. Having dinner with good friends, going on a long, beautiful walk with your family, or watching re-runs on YouTube of politicians falling down steps, then the clock spins by at an exponential rate.

Thanks to my capability for intensive and exhaustive research (yep, Google again), I found out scientists have studied this phenomenon. You'd think they'd have more important matters to be studying such as a cure for Ebola, finding an emissions-free power source or figuring out why the only thing cling film clings to, is itself—but I digress. It appears the old saying, "time flies when you're having fun" has some truth to it.

Time Perception is the phrase used to describe these events, and it is a trick of the brain. When our minds are fully engaged on something, we are not aware of time. On the other hand, when we are listening to upper management talk about increasing stakeholder synergy within a seamless integrated vertical platform, we perceive that time has slowed down or, in my case, going backwards. Why? Because we are now acutely aware of time. We look at our watches or the clock on the wall and think, "I must change jobs", "My God, this guy is a boring tit", or "I really must check my tyre pressure on the way home".

Some of you will be wondering why I brought this subject up. Others will be looking at their watches thinking, "Yep, he's right, time has definitely slowed down. I could swear I've been reading this rubbish for at least two hours, but in fact, it's only twenty seconds."

A few weeks ago I woke up in the morning (duh!), lay in bed, and recalled an event that happened to me over thirty years ago. I went to a nightclub and met a girl. This girl was the most beautiful creature on the planet... *disclaimer*: until I met my future wife, of course. (*Watch it Northouse, you're on shaky ground*—Ed). She was super posh (the mystery girl, not the missus) and her father was a prominent politician at the time. Her family was rich, powerful, and privileged. I, on the other hand, was an apprentice bricklayer and all-round shit-kicker from a rough part of Leeds. We had absolutely nothing in common and at first, she wouldn't even give me the time of day. However, being a persistent young chap and a randy bugger, to boot, I kept chipping away until her facade finally cracked. We talked for hours and there was a chemistry between us. I finally left, alone, and our paths never crossed again. Not once, in the intervening years, has my mind thought about her, until a few weeks back.

Why, after all this time, would that memory resurface? I idly wondered what might have happened had we started a relationship. Within minutes, I was up and away and my next book was being played out like a film in my head. For the following two days, I was in a complete reverie.

I hung a basket of dirty washing out on the line, brought a clean batch in, and put it in the washing machine. I fed the dog cat food and the cat dog food. The dog didn't give a toss; in fact, she seemed to enjoy the change. The cat, however, is still sulking with me to this day. I put sugar in my tea, which I haven't done for twenty years. I forgot to pick my daughter up from netball training. I called my wife, Alan, on at least two occasions, at one point completely forgot the names of my daughters and referred to them as "thingamabob" and "whatshername" for a few hours. One day, I was parked outside the supermarket wondering why my car door wouldn't open. The answer soon became obvious—it wasn't my car—it wasn't even the same model or colour!

Those two days felt like a few brief hours—my mind was completely absorbed with my story and nothing else.

All the females in my life are great at multi-tasking. They can bake bread, fill out their child's excursion form, talk to their friend on the phone, repaint the bathroom ceiling, and memorise all the lyrics to Adele's "Someone Like You", all at the same time, without missing a beat. Their brains are like multiple ring-roads with never-ending forks and side routes, all interweaving and overlapping.

Most of the men I know cannot multi-task. On the odd occasions I've tried to, it ends up a right bloody shambles! I once tried to reconcile my bank statement whilst holding a conversation with my wife and writing a letter to my mother. My wife gave up on the conversation within seconds as she said I was speaking a newly invented language called "utter crap". My mother received a stiff missive from me ranting about bank fees and my bank manager got a very moving letter from me telling him how much I missed and loved him and how was the cat and Mrs Brown's lumbago. Most disturbingly, I received a response from him asking me if I was available for drinks on Friday night followed by a candlelit dinner. Oh, and don't forget to bring my overnight bag!

Men's brains only have one road. It's a six-lane superhighway that travels from the frontal lobe right to the back cortex. Traffic can only flow in one direction and there are no turnoffs or slip-roads. Three of the lanes are reserved specifically for sexual thoughts, two lanes for sport and food, and the last lane for everything else. It's always been a mystery to me that most of the powerful institutions in the world and big business are run by men —no wonder the world is stuffed! Give the job to a handful of multi-tasking women and we'd have peace, love, and prosperity for all, overnight. Anyway, I digress slightly—back to my reverie.

I sat down and began to write. I had everything in my head and needed to get it down on paper as quickly as possible. I figured I had one full-length novel of between 80 to 100k words and a prequel novella of about 30k words. After four days, I had 28k words and had hardly begun to scratch the surface. I realised I needed to do some planning, something I rarely do when writing. I got a large A2 sized art pad and drew a circle on it. For each chapter, I drew a line extending away from the edge of the circle and wrote a brief sentence describing the scene and the characters in it. After thirty minutes, I was done. There were now three full-length novels sketched out.

I'd begin writing at 9 am and would take a break after a couple of hours, but it wasn't two hours that had passed, it was four or five hours. Time had flown. I'd break off about 6 pm to make dinner for Alan, "whatshername" and "thingamabob" and once dinner was done, I was back to the keyboard.

The story is about the young couple who met in that nightclub all those years ago. It is set in 1984, just before the start of the miners' strike (for those of you who are unaware, the miners' strike of '84 were one of the most divisive periods in modern British history). It's a lot more serious than my previous books, (although there are still plenty of laughs going on). It is set to a backdrop of political unrest, mistrust, a young man trying to make his mark on the world and a band of close-knit friends. However, primarily it is a love story. It's even got a few sex scenes in it. These are not there for crass titillation, as having read them back, there is very little titillating going on. They are not graphic, or pornographic, things are sort of alluded to rather than described in detail. The purpose of them is to show the intensity and passion of the relationship.

This is not a lovey-dovey, rosy coloured romance that ends with everyone living happily ever after. It is raw, passionate, pulsating, and realistic. It reminds me of those classic black and white films from the early sixties, which were based on novels by the "Angry Young Man" brigade. Films like "Saturday Night Sunday Morning", "A Room At The Top", "Billy Liar" and "A Kind Of Loving" to name but a few. Don't get me wrong, it is not bleak. In fact, it is quite heart-warming really, and it clicks along at a good pace.

As mentioned earlier, I was born and raised in Yorkshire. Now, the Yorkshire folk can be called many things, and often are, but we are not the most emotive people in the world. The only time a man may shed a tear is when his football team loses or someone knocks his pint over. Our women folk only cry when one of their favourite characters from a soap opera is killed off. Okay, that's not quite true—but you get my drift.

However, writing the book has had me choking up occasionally (come on, I'm not going to admit I cry). Maybe I've found finally found my feminine side. Then in the next chapter, I would laugh like a drain. I know it is not good protocol to laugh at one's own jokes, but reading the words back, it was as if someone else had written them.

The most disturbing thing is I've fallen head-over-heels in love with the protagonist's girlfriend! It's insane, but I cannot stop thinking about her. I know the colour of her hair, her eyes, the way she talks, the way she moves, her funny little sayings—I am besotted with the girl. When my wife asks me how the book is coming along, I get all defensive and secretive.

"Why? What are you implying, don't you trust me? There's absolutely nothing going on. Check my phone if you like." She gazes at me, sadly, as though I'm bonkers. How can a man fall in love with a figment of his own imagination? It's unhealthy, unwise, and bloody unhelpful! I may need therapy after I finish the last book.

For me, it feels like only a couple of days ago since I finished my last newsletter and hit the send button, but it is, in fact, 23 days ago. The next few months are going to fly by and soon I will be sporting 3-inch-long fingernails and nasal hair dangling over my top lip.

So, back to my original point about there being something wrong with the universe. Wouldn't you think the laws of nature or even our own brains would have turned things the opposite way around? Instead of it feeling like it takes three hours to unpack the shopping and unclog the drain, it should whizz by in seconds. The beautiful family day spent at the beach, which flew by in less than an hour, should seem like twenty hours. The dull should go fast and the enjoyable should go slow. If it did, I would have finished my three books by now. Maybe when the universe finally stops expanding and begins to contract, things will reverse, and the good times will seem to last forever, and the bad days will vanish in seconds. It's a nice dream to have.

Chapter 8

Work... What Is It Good For?

Work, what is it good for? Good God, y'all! Don't say, absolutely nothing!

Of course, work is good for something. Money, for one thing, and for getting things done. Without work, there would be no society. However, I must be honest with you; I spent more years than I care to recollect working for a multinational company as a technical writer. I can say, without doubt, this was the most boring time of my life. I know you think life in the Northouse homestead would be one big roller coaster ride of laughs, witty asides, humorous anecdotes, and mindless good humour. Well, you'd be right, that's exactly what it's like when I'm not home, but sometimes we all have to do boring things. Boring things bore me, oddly enough, and I try to put the boring stuff off for as long as possible. Where am I going with this? I really have no idea. (*Surprise, surprise—Ed*).

This brings me neatly onto the word "manager"

"Hang on, how did he extrapolate manager from that?"

Keep up, you at the back. Work / boring things /manager—you see the connection? No? Okay, well don't worry, it's all explained in this month's mildly interesting fact.

When I worked at the multinational company for excruciatingly dull things, I remember a discussion I had with one of my female colleagues. She had taken exception to the word "manager," unlike me, who had taken exception to the "actual" manager. She believed the word was sexist and the title "manager" should be renamed as People and Workflow Coordinator. I know, pretty snappy, eh?

I like words, the sound of them, the look of them on paper and some words make me all happy inside. Words like flabbergasted, discombobulated, Hessian, flibbertigibbet, contumely, and brake fluid. You're thinking the last one is odd, right? It's a contradiction in terms. Brake—meaning to stop and fluid for motion. Amazing!

When my colleague complained about the word, "manager" I decided to do some research (yes, I'm odd). Unfortunately, Google did not exist in those days so I had to use something the young 'uns will never have heard of; Netscape Navigator, which was a bit like Google on elephant tranquillisers.

My colleague wrongly assumed the man in manager referred to the male of the human species and was therefore sexist. However, it has nothing to do with men, or man, or males. Manager derives from the Latin word "manus" *(always with the Latin—Ed)*. It means "hand" and the Italian word "maneggiare" means to control. So, a manager is a hand controller, which sounds a bit dodgy, but Latin is a strange language.

During my time at Purgatory Inc, there were three things I despised: meetings, team-bonding days and the Christmas party. In fact, I actually developed a phobia of meetings but there was no Latin medical term for the condition, so I had to invent my own.

'Jerkocircophobia' (@Simon Northouse, 1999) means a morbid and irrational fear of meetings.

There are a finite number of hours in everyone's lives and wasting those precious hours listening to Kevin from OH&S waffle on about the dangers of lacerating your jugular vein with a paper cut or impaling oneself on a hole punch can seem rather inconsequential.

I'm quite proud of the word "Jerkocircophobia" and please, feel free to use it—there's no charge. In fact, bear with me; I'm going to Google it to make sure it has not been coined by anyone else. Nope, all good, there's plenty of things about jerk circles, whatever they are, but definitely no 'Jerkocircophobia.'

Now, don't misunderstand me, I'm not against meetings per se. Philosophically, I can appreciate their importance. In fact, while I've been in meetings, I've often used the time to ponder how, why and when meetings first entered the human psyche. They were obviously once important.

I can well understand the elders of the tribe getting together every Monday morning to discuss vexing issues that faced their clan. A meeting would be very handy should someone catch wind the neighbouring village of cannibals are planning a surprise attack during the tribe's weekly bath night. Concerns could be aired, plans could be made, delegation of authority could be handed down, minutes taken, and fears allayed. Likewise, if a rogue sabre-toothed tiger was on the prowl, gobbling up little children and the hard of hearing, a meeting would be beneficial to decide how to deal with the errant feline.

Meetings may have been convened for more mundane matters, such as, "Please, could the Attack and Pillage Committee remind their team members to carry their spears upright at all times when not in battle. Last week, we had three near-miss incidents, which could have resulted in a blinding, a partial circumcision, and an unnecessary colonoscopy."

Alas, the modern meeting is very different. Why? Because they are mainly a waste of your time, a stage for those with nothing to say to hold court. The problem with any group gathering which encourages the attendees to air their views and ideas is that, unfortunately, they invariably do. I'm not sure whether meetings are the same the world over (and I suspect they are) but the meetings I had the misfortune to attend were populated with half-wits, the clinically insane, pathological egocentrics, narcissists, the hard of understanding, the proactively disenfranchised,

Dodgy Dave and worst of all, middle management. I include myself in the list—guess which one I was?

Not once in the thousands of meetings I attended over the years did a meeting begin on time. Not only that, but I could count on the fingers of a one-fingered hand how many times I left a meeting and thought to myself, "Hmm, that was productive."

I had nothing against getting together with a few colleagues during the week to discuss some pressing issues like why are so many people spelling the word "specific" as "pacific"? Or why do people insist on capitalising common nouns? I know, riveting, right?

One day, I received an email from my manager stating all meetings were now mandatory to attend. I don't know about you, but I hate being told what to do. It's an anti-authority thing I've had since I was a child. Don't worry, I'm not a homicidal maniac—honest.

I spoke earlier about words I love. I also have a list of words I hate, such as; vagary, ballcock, cloche, Switzerland, clamp, hither and mandatory—to name but a few. From that day on, I never attended another meeting. People worried for me, "You must attend, it's mandatory." No, it's not bloody mandatory! It's mandatory I keep to the speed limit. It's mandatory I pay my income tax. It's mandatory I don't drive when I'm over the limit and it's mandatory I remove my toenail clippings from the bathroom sink when I've finished! However, it is not mandatory I attend a pointless meeting!

From that day on, I never attended another meeting, and guess what? The world kept turning. My productivity soared, which in turn made my manager look good, so he turned a blind eye to me not attending his mandatory meetings (that were not mandatory).

I have a very simple outlook to work. It is a business contract between an employer and an employee or contractor. As an employee, I do the work the employer wants me to do, and they pay me for the hours I work. I give my time—they give me money in return. If, after a month, they realise I am good at my job, they keep giving me more work and they keep paying me. They're happy and I'm unhappy, but at least I'm paying the bills and putting food on the table for my family. It is a simple and easily understood coalition.

If, after a month, they realise I'm totally feckless and incompetent at my job—then the solution is simple—they promote me to a managerial role in another department and are rid of me. This is how it used to work. But things changed in the nineties—and I blame the Americans! (*Watch it boyo, most of your readers are from LaLaLand—Ed.*)

In the nineties, the world was inundated with feel-good, self-help, time management, leadership, and how to get-rich-quick books written by white-middle-aged-American men. I am actually embarrassed to admit I read a few of those books.

They were always the same. They sold the idea you could be whatever you wanted to be by simply visualising it. Sorry, but that is complete codswallop! (Another noble word.) Visualising something in your head does not make it happen. If it did, I would have spent many a long and happy night with Nicole Kidman, Demi Moore, and Angela Lansbury in a dungeon (don't ask, it's complicated).

Thought must be married with action to achieve anything. There is a time for thinking and a time for doing, and I do not need a guy whose smile could blind you from a thousand paces to tell me that.

Which brings me back to meetings, "It does?" Yes, it does. Please keep up!

The failure of most meetings is they are people's thought bubbles. Thoughts are spoken, and that's it. There is rarely any doable action to be undertaken after the thought bubble has passed. Meetings are the refuge of those who do not have enough work to do; of those who like the sound of their own voice, and of those who like to feel important even though they realise they're not. So, my advice would be, if you want to achieve something, think about it, then put those thoughts into action, and keep away from bloody meetings, they'll suck the life out of you!

If you can feel my antipathy towards meetings, then wait until the next newsletter when I smite down the biggest waste of time of any workplace activity—Team-Bonding. Even the words send me into a cold sweat.

Next month I will recount the one and only time I attended a team-bonding day. It was about as enjoyable as my visit to a proctologist with fingers the size of cucumbers and a poor sense of humour! Never a good mix, in my humble opinion.

Chapter 9

Team-Bonding

I 've been busy this last month putting the finishing touches to the third book in the Shooting Star series, Fall Of A Shooting Star. It was 80% complete about six months ago, but the last 20% has been a real ball-ache. There were a few plot holes that needed tidying up. The trouble is, when writing, once you change something after the event, it has a knock-on effect throughout the entire book. It's like throwing a pebble into a pond and seeing the ripples expand forever outwards.

I did what any talented writer would do *(presumption, my friend, presumption—Ed)* and I avoided it. After all, a problem ignored is a problem solved. At one stage it got so bad I tackled all the other problems I've been avoiding, to avoid finishing the book. I cleaned my office, removed leaves from the gutters, cut the grass even though there's nothing to cut. I even got into a long conversation with the bloke on duty at the council tip, something I'd vowed never to do again after my last harrowing experience. He's a nice enough chap, but he's had a personality transplant and he makes watching grass grow seem like an extreme sport.

However, I finally knuckled down and am now racing towards the finishing line at the speed of a glacier. Okay, let's get on with it *(my thoughts exactly—Ed.)*

Oxytocin? Does anyone know what it is? (Okay, well done you over there. There's always a smartarse lurking in the background). I'll be honest with you; I had no idea what it was until I stumbled upon some interesting research into team-bonding (I told you I've been avoiding finishing my book).

To me, oxytocin sounds like one of those high-fibre bedtime drinks for people with a sluggish bowel. However, it's not. It is actually a chemical released by the brain during sexual orgasm *(is there any other type of orgasm—Ed.)* Research conducted by IPRAFT (Institute of Pointless Research Again Funded by the Taxpayer) found this same chemical is released during team-bonding days. *WTF! GET OUT OF HERE!* I kid you not.

I'm not exactly sure what team-bonding games were being played at the time the research was being conducted, but it certainly didn't reflect my team-bonding experiences. I can honestly state, with hand on heart, there was no oxytocin released from my brain during our team-building days. Melatonin, yes, but oxytocin, no.

Bigas Vinculum is Latin for team-bonding. I know it sounds like a vulgar term for a certain part of the female anatomy, but that's Latin for you. Now, I'm no scholar, *(really? I wouldn't have guessed—Ed)* but I'm pretty sure the Romans didn't take part in many meetings or team-bonding sessions, otherwise, they'd never have moved further than the walls of Rome. Although, I suppose ransacking and pillaging is a form of team-bonding if you're into that sort of caper. The Romans were action men (and women). They'd look at a map of Europe or North Africa and say, 'Yep, we'll have Gaul this week and next month I fancy a holiday in Crete. Let's do it!'

As middle and upper management are wont to do, one year during my stint at Purgatory Inc, they thought it would be a splendid idea to send our department on a Bigas Vinculum day.

Come the big day, a coach drove our group of eighteen to the Stalag, where we began our bonding session. The first thing our team-bonding "mentor" did was to split us up into six teams of three. I did bring to the mentor's attention that splitting the group up was the opposite of what team-bonding was about. I could tell from the hatred in his eyes he saw me as a troublemaker—too bloody right!

For sins from a previous life, I was grouped with Hypochondriac Harry and Numerical Norman. Harry was a decent bloke but his drain on the health system was greater than the GDP of some third-world countries. I have empathy. I have sympathy. I am not immune to the suffering of my fellow man or woman. But, when you've listened to Harry for fifteen minutes each day of your working life, describe his ailments to you, then... well, your empathy diminishes somewhat. To listen about the inner workings (or outer) of his irritable bowel first thing on a Monday morning is not the best start to a week. I'd have been irritable if I'd been Harry's bowel.

As for Numerical Norman, he was head of accounts. He was a dull-witted chap who suffered from halitosis, rampaging dandruff, and worst of all, an appalling dress sense. I'm sure his grandmother dressed him each day. I'm unsure if there's a word for it, but he had the equivalent of numerical dyslexia. I found this out after my first month on the job when I checked my bank balance. To my immense pleasure, I noticed I'd been paid £120'000 for a month's work. I was bloody good at my job, and to be honest, worth every cent, but something told me there had been a foul-up in accounts. The foul-up was Norman, one of many foul-ups. Of course, I ended up paying the money back, begrudgingly.

The following month, I received no payment at all. After two weeks of investigation, it was revealed my wage had gone to a Mr Unbutoo in Nigeria, for which I am sure he was eternally grateful. He withdrew all the money, closed his bank account and was last seen in a drunken stupor, stumbling around the streets of Abuja singing "Girls Just Wanna Have Fun" by Cyndi Lauper. With the power of hindsight, I wish I had done the same (apart from the choice of song). Anyway, I digress. Back to team-bonding.

Our glorious "mentor" set us all our first team-bonding task. He placed in front of us a plastic straw, a paper clip, a rubber band and asked us to construct a replica of the Eiffel Tower. Apparently, it took ten minutes of CPR, a dozen zaps from a defibrillator, a good whiff of Mrs Bandy's Miraculous Sniffing Salts and a dose of Dr Gripes Nerve Syrup to bring me around. When I finally resumed my seat, I set to the task with gusto. Harry and Norman were about as much use as tits on a bull, so I knew I'd have to sail the ship alone. We'd been allocated ten minutes to complete the task. After thirty seconds, I was done and informed the mentor. He studied my masterpiece for a few nanoseconds and didn't look impressed. Granted, to the naked eye, it may have looked like a plastic straw with a paper clip attached to it with the aid of a rubber band. However, as I explained to him, he was looking at it through a physical prism. He needed to view it through the metaphysical eye. After all, art is subjective. We came last.

I'm not sure what unfolded for the next two hours because I said I had an urgent dental appointment and escaped. In fact, having a root canal would have been preferable to spending another minute in the team-bonding Gulag.

I returned at 2 pm, hoping the day was all but over. What a naïve, foolish innocent abroad I was. As we all trooped onto the coach, our mentor informed us we were all about to have some "great fun". His words sent a shiver down my spine. He informed us we were heading to the Croquet Club. I desperately ransacked my lunchbox looking for my cyanide pills. Alas, my dear wife had forgotten to pack them that particular day. Numerical Norman idly informed me his mother was good at knitting. I was grateful for this piece of information and will now die a happy man.

For those lucky few who don't know what croquet is, I'll explain. British toffs invented croquet to pass the time away. When they weren't busy invading other countries, shooting peasants, or groping their housemaids, they needed something to occupy their minds. Being well educated, to the manor-born and naturally ingenious, they put their collective heads together and came up with the game of croquet.

It basically involves bending a coat hanger into a "U" shape and sticking it into the ground. A ball, about three inches in diameter, is then whacked through the hoops with a mallet you've borrowed from your gardener. There are no points and no rules, and no one wins or loses. The game ends when news comes through that there's a peasant shoot beginning on Lord Dingletwat's estate at 3 pm—prompt. At this point, the game is abandoned, and everyone tucks into cucumber sandwiches, iced tea, and a good serving of Eton Mess. After high tea, the lady folk retire to their embroidery room to knit teapots and the men don their shooting jackets and get their butler to piggyback them to Lord Dingletwat's estate, twelve miles away.

Thankfully, our game of croquet came to an abrupt, and disturbing halt when Hypochondriac Harry had a giddy turn while attempting to extricate his mallet from an elderly lady who had been bent over doing a spot of weeding nearby. He was lucky to escape being put on the sex-offenders register.

At the start of the day, we had been a bunch of co-workers, tolerant and accepting of each other's strengths and weaknesses. By the end of the day, we were six disparate teams of three. Hating, sniping, and vowing revenge on each other for the rest of eternity. Hmm, team-bonding, indeed.

Chapter 10

Genre, Genre, Genre

Have you ever had one of those months where you say to yourself, "What a hell of a month!"

Well, that's been my month. There's been the good, the bad, and the fugly.

I've attended a wedding, been on a long road trip with my family, had the clutch go in my car, had the gearbox go in my wife's car, spent a night in gaol, had the air-con for the house give up the ghost, suffered from a swollen finger and found a foreign body in my pasta.

"Hang on a mo!" I can hear you cry, "back-up a bit... you spent a night where?" Yes, in gaol. I found it quite pleasant, although the rest of the family were less than impressed, as we did all have to share a cell together.

Family holidays are always stressful. As I explained to my kids, family getaways are not meant to be enjoyed at the time they happen. No, it's only upon returning home, unpacking, and allowing a few days to pass, before we can all look back fondly on our time together. By then we have forgotten about the bitch-fights in the car, the spiders, and rats in the gaol cell, the short-curly hair loitering with malevolent intent in my linguine, and the slack-jawed moron who nearly ran us off the road. Ah, great times.

Anyway, enough twaddle; let us move on to this month's Mildly Interesting Fact. I'm a writer, (stop sniggering), so I deal with words. I like to know their meaning *(always helpful... being a writer—Ed)* and I like to investigate their origin and how they evolved. Therefore, this month, I'm looking at the word "Genre" and for good reason, although that reason may not be obvious at first, or even ever.

Genre is a French word, meaning "sort, style, kind" and is related to the word "gender". But as with most things, everything comes back to Latin. The French language was based on Latin. Okay, that sounds low brow. The French people didn't wake up one day and say, "Hey, Pierre, I have a great idea, why don't we invent a new language based on Latin? We'll call it French!" No, language evolves over time.

Latin was the official language of the Romans, and as we know, the Romans liked to get about a bit. Think of them as the Russian tourists of today, but not as aggressive. The Romans loved Europe, North Africa, and the Middle East. In fact, they liked it so much they kept it, well, for a time at least. They went as far north as northern England then stopped, which was odd, as the Romans weren't the stopping type. However, on reflection, if you've ever spent a winter in Scotland (or a summer) you'd understand why—however—I digress.

The French word Genre can be traced back to the Latin word Genus (there is no "I" in Genus) and Genus means birth, race, kind, and sort. In short, it's a classification word.

As an aside, if you left the letter "E" out of Genus you'd have a herd of wildebeest rampaging through your newsletter right now *(you're digressing again—get on with it! Ed)*

Okay, so what is the point of all this? *(Good question—Ed.)* Well, it's all about genre, something which is very important to a writer. It's the equivalent of location, location, location, to a real estate agent.

For the few who haven't already hit the unsubscribe button with a certain amount of zeal, read on.

Books are classified into genres, and I often ask myself what "genre" I write in. I have four completely different series published at the moment.

The Shooting Star series, Soul Love series, The School Days series and this twaddle I'm writing now—The Discombobulated Newsletter series.

None of them are easy to classify as they are not written to market. They are not mystery although there is some mystery in the first two series. They are not romance, but there is romance in the Soul Love series along with a bit of paranormal. There are varying amounts of humour (or attempts at humour) in all the books, but humour is not a standalone genre. It makes them damned hard to market, and I always end dumping them in the satire/parody/comedy categories on Amazon.

It would be nice if the powers-that-be invented a new genre called, "A bit of everything," or "Omni-genre." When asked, "what genre are you?" I could confidently reply, "Omni-genre."

Parody is used as a device to imitate and mock someone or something. It is designed to make one laugh or at least smile. Satire is slightly different. It uses humour mixed with varying degrees of anger or frustration to make a point. Great parody should make you laugh. Great satire should make you think. Satire is a great tool for a writer as it gives us a chance to let a character show their true colours without the author bludgeoning the reader with a statement of fact. I'll give a quick example from a new book that I'm writing at the moment.

The character, Joe, is in his late fifties and basically, he's sexist against women. He is not a misogynist, he does not hate women, but deep down he believes in the old-fashioned values of men being in charge. However, he would never admit to this, as he wants to be seen as a reasonable and modern thinking man. In my book, I could have simply said, "It was plain to see that Joe was sexist, despite his protestations." That's okay, it makes its point, and the reader is left in no doubt about Joe. However, instead, I used a bit of satire to weave more colour into the paragraph and to let Joe show us he is sexist. The excerpt below involves a conversation between Joe and the protagonist, Jimmy (who is aged twenty).

"I believe women, girls, should be treated exactly like men. They should have the same opportunities that are available to men. Unfortunately, there is a lot of ingrained sexism in our society," said Jimmy with a fire in his belly. Joe sat down in his special chair and stared at Jimmy for a moment.

"Quite right, young man. I couldn't agree more," Joe replied thoughtfully. "Darling?" he called out to his wife. "Did you iron my white shirt yet? I am due at the club in an hour. Oh, and while you're in the kitchen, would you put the kettle on and make me a cup of tea, there's a dear."

This brief excerpt tells us way more about Joe than the first, matter-of-fact statement. We know Joe has a chair, his chair that no one else is presumably allowed to sit in. Joe is King, the chair, his throne. He's incapable of ironing his own shirt as he doesn't know how to—he's never done it before. His wife is in the kitchen, apparently in her domain. He asks for a cup of tea. He doesn't offer to make a cup of tea for Jimmy or his wife. He's also rather patronising, referring to Jimmy as "young man", and using the phrase "there's a dear" to his wife. Now, that paragraph is more "wry" than funny, but by using satire, Joe has shown us his true colours.

There are many phrases in the English language that describe someone who brings about their own downfall. One of my favourites was used by Shakespeare, "hoist with his own petard". A petard is an old word for a small bomb. Hoist means to go up. Therefore, blown up by one's own bomb. The phrase these days is used to mean brought down by one's own words or deeds.

Satire doesn't have to be laugh-out-loud funny. In fact, I find the best satire is the type that makes me smile and wince at the same time. When this happens, I know the writer has hit the nail on the head.

Chapter 11

Misinterpretation

As I write this, it is exactly 50 years ago today since one of the greatest moments in the history of humanity (and womankind) occurred. Yes, you guessed it, "Give Peace A Chance" by John Lennon and the Plastic Ono Band, peaked at number 2 in the UK singles charts, a travesty of justice as it should have hit the top spot.

For any millennials who are a bit bamboozled by the above statement, let me explain. A "single" was a round piece of vinyl, 7 inches in diameter that was placed on a machine called a record player. The single spun around and when a needle was placed on top of it, music came out of a speaker. Furthermore, you had to walk to a record shop and purchase a record with money if you wanted to listen to music. I know, it sounds archaic and ridiculous, doesn't it? Wait, stop: I'm being facetious, fatuous, frivolous.

This is the problem with the written word. It is easy for the reader to misinterpret the author's true intent. For all of you familiar with my monthly ramblings, you know this newsletter is a bit of fun, tongue-in-cheek, irreverent, and as one person informed me, "bloody long-winded." This same person also told me they didn't have time to read because they were too busy. I understand, I really do. This email is not intended to be read when you're frantically strapping the kids into the car, mowing the lawn or de-sexing your neighbour's ferrets. It is to be perused at leisure, during a coffee break or in the office when you're supposed to be working. People can stop and start at will or choose not to read it at all.

Last month I received an email from a person who wasn't just angry, they were bloody livid! They said they had never signed up for the newsletter and my jokes were lame, and as payback for this infringement of liberty, they were going to sock it to me, by unsubscribing. I know my jokes are lame; some of them should be on life support. As for not signing up for my newsletter, that is a different kettle of turnips. Everyone must go through the process of signing up for it, either on a book promo site or from my website. There is no other way I could know your email address.

I wondered why the person in question, didn't simply hit unsubscribe and be done with it. They felt the need to give me a "bloody nose" as they exited, which is fine. Better to have a go at me than kick the cat. All of this brings me neatly on to this month's Mildly Interesting Fact.

Ira Illud, (as text-rage is called in Latin) is a modern-day phenomenon. Apparently, it is most common when dealing with emails. People who have a short fuse and expect their modern-day communications to be concise and snappy can get bloody annoyed when confronted with a communique that is longer than a telephone number. Also, because the email is a one-way street, i.e. only the sender is talking, people can feel disempowered.

Not only that, but it is easy to misinterpret the sender's true intent. The reader may think they are being patronised or insulted. They may regard the email as hostile or passive-aggressive because there is no one-on-one communication. When we talk face to face with someone, we can tell by the tone of their voice or facial expressions what their true intent is. In fact, in situations like these, words are almost secondary, as we pick up cues from body language. There's now a whole lexicon of words that have "rage" as a suffix or a prefix.

Page-rage: I'll put my hand up to this one. I suffer from this all the time. The official description is of someone who leaves nasty reviews on social media or websites. I don't do that, but I do suffer from an offshoot of page-rage. You know when you're reading a terrible book, *(I'm sure your readers know exactly what you mean—Ed)* but you persist with it night after night in the hope it will get better... and it doesn't. Then one night, after a particularly atrocious split-infinitive, followed immediately by a dangling modifier, you launch the book at the wall. Yes, there's many a famous author who has face-planted into my plasterboard.

Rage-clean: Bit of a misnomer, this one. It doesn't mean to clean up in a state of extreme anger. It takes "rage" as an informal verb. It means to clean quickly. The type of cleaning you do when your wife has been hard at work all day and you've been binge watching "The Walking Dead" on Netflix while digesting ten packets of Cheezels. You look around the house and realise it's a bombsite. You notice the clock and say, "Blood and thunder! My sweetness and light will be home in ten minutes. Time for a rage-clean."

You run around like a headless chicken, throwing anything not nailed down into the shoe cupboard. You vac the floor, polish the cat, and start the dishwasher—even though there's nothing in it. Finally, you pull all the curtains shut and lower the lighting just in time. When she asks what I've been up to all day, I reply, with exhausted weariness,

"Haven't bloody stopped cleaning all day, love. I'm worn out." Oh, yes, I've been there many times. In fact, I'll be doing a rage-clean as soon as I've finished this newsletter.

Rage-buy: It happens all the time. Those instances when you are forced to buy something imperative to your well-being. It could be a new set of tyres for your car. A replacement air-conditioner before the onset of a blisteringly hot summer, or a three pack of Calvin Klein underpants. You don't want to buy them, but you must. To rub salt into the wound, the article in question is so expensive it gives you a nosebleed. You know you are being shafted but there's nothing you can do about it because it is an essential item. So begins rage-buy. You deliberately pick a fight with the shop assistant, scream, "What are you staring at?" to a small child, then jump in the car, shaking with rage-buy which quickly morphs into road-rage.

Whine-rage: My daughters, and occasionally my wife, suffer from this condition, *(ooh, you're a brave man, Northouse... or stupid—Ed)*. When I pick my girls up after work or a school excursion, I am the recipient of whine-rage. My God, they can carry on! You'd assume they were living in a third-world country, wearing rags, and ravished with hunger. The weather's too hot or too cold, the school trip was boring, they didn't enjoy the caramel flambé in their lunchbox; they weren't allowed their smartphones on the coach. If there were a world championship for never-ending whining, my two would be serious contenders. When they're both in the car at the same time, I get stereophonic whingeing. It's at times like these I visit my special place, deep inside my head.

Rage-cancel: This occurs when you are purchasing something online. For reasons best known to itself, the transaction is taking longer than expected. At 5 seconds you become annoyed. After 10 seconds you are seething and after 20 seconds you are in a sweaty, uncontrollable rage. Your only recourse for this injustice? To cancel the order. Welcome to rage-cancel.

Rage-decorating: This is something I have been guilty of in the past. When we are expecting visitors coming to stay with us, my wife suddenly becomes all house-proud. It doesn't seem to bother her we live in squalor for the other 51 weeks of the year. She gives me a list of jobs to do. Repaint the front room, fix the back door, stain the deck, weed the garden and bitumen the bathroom ceiling, oh, and don't forget to fix the hole in the plasterboard you made when you threw Jeffrey Archer at it the other night. I complete my chores with gritted teeth raging inside.

Queue-rage: Being British, I never suffer queue-rage. As you know, the Brits invented queuing as a way to pass the time of day until something more interesting came along. We queue in silence, well aware of the grand order of things. Without orderly queuing, what have you got? Chaos, that's what! As my next-door neighbour, René Descartes, once said, "I queue, therefore I am." A bit of a thinker is old René, although he's not the sort of person you'd invite to a party to liven things up. To the Brits, the most heinous crime you can commit is to queue jump. There's a special place in hell for those types.

Air-rage: I'm sure most people have at least witnessed this. There's nothing worse... well, apart from queue jumpers, of course. There's always some cock-muppet who has to have a pop at the air hostess. He may well be a vegetarian with a violent allergic reaction to peanuts, but there's no need to go off like a pork chop because he's been served skewered satay chicken for lunch. Suck it up, big boy, and move on. Of course, this is actually a combination of air-rage and food-rage.

Food-rage: You've seen him, I've seen him—the guy in the restaurant who wants to draw attention to himself, because of feelings of inadequacy. Now he plans to stuff up everyone's evening by acting like a baby who hasn't slept for 24 hours and is teething. There's always something wrong with the meal. The meat's too rare or it's overdone. The ice cream isn't cold enough, the coffee is not the correct shade of black, the water's too wet. Even if a trio of 3-star, Michelin chefs, made up of Marco Pierre White, Gordon Ramsay, and Kanye West, served up a plate of Japanese Wagyu steak with truffle sauce, infused with saffron, this guy would complain the decor was not to his liking. Talking of Kanye West, for years I assumed it was Aldi's home-brand tuna until my daughter enlightened me.

Actually, you may find this hard to believe, but I was once the instigator of a food-rage incident, *(strangely, I can believe it—Ed.)* A couple of years ago I went out for a meal with my wife and daughters to a fancy-schmancy, super expensive restaurant *(obviously before you were trying to make a living as an author—Ed.)* Can you please shut up! I'm trying to write here!

I ordered oysters for my starter. They arrived with the obligatory lemon quarters to squeeze over them. As I gripped the lemon slice, it suddenly flew from my grip at the speed of a bullet. It shot across the restaurant and hit an elderly gentleman in the neck as he was tucking into his dessert of "distressed peach melba". Don't ask me why his peach melba was distressed. Maybe it had been handed a speeding ticket earlier in the day, or perhaps its partner had desserted them *(oh, dear ... Ed)* but I digress.

The elderly man was less than impressed at being hit in the throat by a piece of citrus. He immediately accused the party sat opposite him of launching the fruit cruise missile. A hell of a ruckus erupted, which quickly spread like wildfire throughout the dining room. Meanwhile, I slurped on my oysters, watching the free entertainment. A fun night was had by all, well, by me at least. Boy, did those oysters taste good, although a tad more lemon juice wouldn't have gone amiss.

Alas, that is the end of this rage-athon. I'm sure as we saunter through the years, more rage suffixes and prefixes will appear. I can already hear a smartphone hitting the wall as someone flies into a newsletter-rage.

Chapter 12

Getting To The Bottom Of Things

A couple of years ago, I had something peculiar going on downstairs. No, I'm not talking about weird noises coming from the cellar. I'm trying to be polite and tactful. Let me say I got a referral to a proctologist. Aha! Now the penny drops—try to keep up.

I'm not particularly fond of doctors, but occasionally, my wife realises I need to see one. It was with resigned truculence I paid a visit to the practice rooms of Dr Menuhin. He was the first proctologist I'd ever seen, and he enjoyed his work a little too much for my liking. I didn't much care for his name either—I suspected he may have been on the fiddle *(just when I thought the lame jokes had finished—Ed.)* However, the most disconcerting fact about him was that he had the hands of a navvy and fingers the size of Lebanese cucumbers.

Dr Menuhin wasn't content to have a good old rummage inside me with his cucumber fingers. Oh no, he wanted to get me into hospital and have a proper go at it. He told me it was a routine procedure that involved sending a camera up inside. It was at this point I had visions of a cameraman dressed in a wetsuit getting oiled up by his assistant. I didn't really want to go into hospital, but once I'd told my wife, I had little choice in the matter.

It was the most humiliating experience of my life! I'm not talking about the actual investigative procedure. I realise going up the rectum is a serious matter and nothing to joke about. What was humiliating was the preoperation routine. I assumed I would be given a private room with my own ensuite, considering certain things had to take place before the camera crew entered me. I consider myself pretty streetwise and clued up, but sometimes I can be a real thicko.

On arrival at the hospital, I sat in an overcrowded waiting room for thirty minutes. Eventually, a nurse appeared brandishing a clipboard. In a voice, which I'm confident was heard by all aboard the International Space Station, she yelled,

'Mr Northouse? Colonoscopy?' The crowded waiting room, which, until that point, had been a sombre tomb of boredom, now bristled with excitement. I hurriedly followed the nurse out of the room and into the hospital ward. Nope, no private room for me. She pointed to a bed on the end of a lengthy line of beds and said,

'Please get undressed and put the gown on and I'll be back in ten minutes.' I looked to my right and there was a row of reclining chairs occupied by people in various states of discombobulation. It was the post-operation recovery room. Some gawped at me with vacant expressions, wondering what time the film would begin. Others happily munched on egg sandwiches, and one or two looked like they needed urgent medical assistance. Directly opposite my bed was the door to the waiting room, a door that was wide open. A row of faces stared at me, waiting for a bit of free entertainment. I drew the curtains around my bed and disrobed. No sooner had I got my gown on and the nurse was back.

'Mr Northouse,' she barked at me, 'your gown is on back to front. The opening should be at the back.' Well, how was I to know, although considering the exploratory investigation I was about to undergo, it made sense.

'Ah! Okay,' I replied. 'If you could pop outside, I'll put it on the other way around.' The nurse huffed at this.

'Nonsense. You haven't got anything I haven't seen a million times before,' she responded impatiently. I felt like saying, "Okay, why don't you get your kit off, don't worry love, you've nothing I haven't seen before." However, the nurse was a woman of senior years, and I wasn't sure if that statement would hold water. Turning my back to her, I pulled the robe off and was about to put it on the correct way when I heard the swish of the curtains. The nurse was heading off down the corridor and had left the curtains open. Fascinated faces ogled my nakedness from the confines of the waiting room. I quickly pulled the curtains shut, put the robe on, and lay on the bed, contemplating the rich tapestry of life.

A few minutes passed before the nurse returned with a couple of plastic tubes.

'Okay, Mr Northouse, in a few minutes I'll be giving you an enema,' she boomed. 'It should be painless.' I'll be the judge of that, I thought. 'All you'll feel is a cold sensation in the bottom.'

Once again, she buggered off, leaving the curtains open. There was at least one redeeming part to this hospital farce, and it was the fact the nurse was elderly and female. I'm not sure I could have handled an attractive young nurse or God, forbid, a male nurse administering the enema. That may sound ageist or even sexist but I don't mean it like that. The nurse was more of a motherly or even grandmotherly figure, and her air of impatient indifference brought me some solace.

When the nurse returned, she asked me to roll onto my side and pull my knees up and into my chest. I heard the smack of rubber gloves being put on and an unfamiliar voice. I looked over my shoulder to notice another nurse in tow. A young nurse, an attractive young nurse. Strike me down. If it doesn't rain, it pours!

'Now, Mr Northouse, you don't mind if our junior nurse administers the enema, do you? They need to learn somewhere,' shouted the elderly nurse, as though she were working on the docks. Well, what choice did I have? My humiliation was now complete—or so I thought. The nurse was right, and she was wrong. Yes, it was cold, and no, it wasn't bloody painless. With the second tube inserted, rather roughly, in my opinion, I threw a quick glance over my shoulder. The damn curtain was slightly open again. There was now a crowd in the waiting room, all jostling for the best position. I swear I could hear a hawker drumming up business from the street outside.

'Roll up! Roll up! Step this way for the greatest show on earth!'

When the procedure was complete, the nurse informed me I had to keep the liquid in for as long as possible, at least fifteen minutes.

'Where's the toilet?' I asked. The nurse yanked the curtains fully open and pointed across the corridor to a door that backed into the waiting room.

The first couple of minutes were a breeze. By the third minute, there was a definite rumble in the jungle and by minute four, I was performing involuntary Kegels that would have got me a spot on the British Olympic Kegel Team.

I broke out in a cold sweat and realised I had only seconds before imminent disaster! I tentatively lifted myself off the bed and teetered out into the corridor. The problem was, my buttocks were so tightly clenched they could have split the atom. This prevented me from walking normally. The only way I could move was to keep my legs rigid with my feet splayed outwards. As I made my way across the corridor, I caught my reflection in the mirrored glass of the reception. I looked like a cross between an arthritic penguin and Frankenstein's monster.

Thankfully, I made it to the toilet and closed the door behind me. Worried murmurs from the waiting room hung in the air as two people stopped right outside the toilet door to engage in a nice little chat about the weather. There was no way I could hold on any longer.

I'll skip the details, but let's just say seismologists around the globe were frantically examining their seismographs to pinpoint the exact location of the tectonic shift which had occurred in the earth's plates. Tsunami warnings were duly issued for the Pacific Basin.

As I made my way back to the bed, I no longer cared my arse was on view for the world to see. I collapsed onto the bed with blessed relief. But not for long. As with earthquakes, there are often a few pre-tremors before the big one. Unbeknownst to me, the first visit to the lavatory was nothing but a pre-tremor.

The nurse returned and said I was doing well. Eight minutes had elapsed, only seven more to go. I informed her lift-off had already taken place some moments earlier. She looked disappointed in me, as though I'd let the team down. I aired my concerns about safely making a return trip to the toilet and suggested she put the Chemical Spill Team on red alert. I felt another unnatural sensation from down below and fully expected the Alien to erupt out of my midriff at any moment. And my nurse was no Sigourney Weaver. She smiled wearily at me as she handed me a giant nappy.

'Here, put this on,' she ordered. Under normal circumstances, I would have snorted derisively at her. Not on this occasion. The nappy went on in world record time.

I made my way back and forth to the toilet another four times. I walked as though rigor mortis had set in, and each time I passed the waiting room, I silently cursed the smirking faces.

Eventually, the storm abated. The nurse returned and gave me a pre-med and within minutes I was off with the pixies having a wonderful time. As they wheeled me into the operating theatre, I was happily whistling, "Doo Wah Diddy Diddy" by Manfred Man. The camera crew and production team were all waiting, dressed in wetsuits and greased up, but I didn't care anymore.

Lets Keep In Touch

If you enjoyed this book then you have just read the best pieces from my free monthly newsletter. If you wish to keep up to date with my book news, there are a few simple ways to be notified. You can subscribe to my entertaining (subjective) monthly "**Discombobulated**" newsletter. This not only keeps you abreast of new releases, but occasionally I have a free book to giveaway or promotional discounts. The newsletter is designed to entertain, with short, pithy takes on the world and life... mostly my life. There's no hard sell and I won't be inundating you with spammy "buy, buy, buy" nonsense – which I personally detest. You can sign up by following the link below, which will take you to my website.

I would like to subscribe to your newsletter.

Alternatively, you can go to the following sites and click on the "**Follow**" button.

Amazon

BookBub

Facebook

For paperback readers, the links above won't work no matter how many times you tap your finger on the paper. Below is a manual link to type into your browser.

https://www.subscribepage.com/author_simon_northouse_home

If you enjoyed this book, then *reviews* are greatly appreciated. If you wish to contact me, my email address is: **simon@simonnorthouse.com** I enjoy a friendly chat, and will always reply.

Also By Simon Northouse

The Shooting Star Series

Arc Of A Shooting Star (Novel)

The Resurrection Tour Diaries (Short Story)

Catch A Shooting Star (Novel)

Fall Of A Shooting Star (Novel)

What's It All About... Geordie? (Novel)

Nuts At Christmas (Novella)

Eggs Unscrambled (Novel)

I Will Survive (Novel)

Bells At Christmas (Novel) – November 2021

The Soul Love Series

Soul Love (Prequel Novella)

Love Is The Goal (Novel)

Love On A Roll (Novel)

Love Of The Coal (Novel) - Due in 2022

The Discombobulated Newsletter Series

Keep On Keeping On - Book 1 (Novella)

Keep Karma and Carry On - Book 2 (Novella)

The Lockdown Diary Blues - Book 3 (Novella)

Carry On Keeping On - Book 4 (Novella)

Keeping On Again - Boxset/Omnibus Edition - Books 1 - 4 (Novel)

The School Days Series

The School Report - Before We Were Tsars (Novella)

The School Report - The Final Term (Novella)

Printed in Great Britain
by Amazon

23256585R00047